For my father
—A.S.C.

HarperCollins®, ☰®, Harper Trophy®, and I Can Read Book® are trademarks of HarperCollins Publishers Inc.

Library of Congress Cataloging-in-Publication Data is available.
ISBN 978-0-06-117745-3 (trade bdg.) — ISBN 978-0-06-117746-0 (pbk.)
09 10 11 12 13 LP/WOR 10 9 8 7 6 5 4 3 2 ❖ First Edition

I Can Read!

SHARED

My First

READING

Biscuit Takes a Walk

story by ALYSSA SATIN CAPUCILLI
pictures by PAT SCHORIES

HarperCollins*Publishers*

Time for a walk, Biscuit.

Woof, woof!

It's time for a walk
to Grandpa's house.

Let's go!
Woof, woof!

Time for a walk, Biscuit.

Woof, woof!

Biscuit wants to dig.

Time for a walk, Biscuit.

Woof, woof!

Biscuit wants to roll.

Funny puppy!
It's time for a walk
to Grandpa's house.

Let's go!

Woof, woof!

9

Time for a walk, Biscuit.
Woof, woof!
Biscuit wants to see
the squirrels.

Time for a walk, Biscuit.

Woof, woof!

12

Biscuit wants
to see the birds.

Silly puppy!
It's time for a walk
to Grandpa's house.
Woof!

Wait, Biscuit. Come back.

Grandpa's house is this way!

Woof, woof!

Oh, Biscuit!

What do you see now?

Woof, woof!

It's Grandpa!

Woof, woof!

A walk to Grandpa's house

is fun, Biscuit.

But a walk with Grandpa

is the best walk of all.

Time for a walk, Biscuit.

A walk for everyone.

24

Woof, woof!